D0175500

THE CASE OF THE CREEPERS

AN UNOFFICIAL MINECRAFTER MYSTERIES SERIES

BOOK FOUR

WITHDRAWN

THE CASE OF THE CREEPERS

AN UNOFFICIAL MINECRAFTER MYSTERIES SERIES

BOOK FOUR

Winter Morgan

Sky Pony Press
New York

This book is not authorized or sponsored
by Microsoft Corp., Mojang AB, Notch
Development AB or Scholastic Inc., or
any other person or entity owning or
controlling rights in the Minecraft name,
trademark, or copyrights.

Copyright © 2018 by Hollan Publishing, Inc.

Minecraft® is a registered trademark of Notch Development AB.

The Minecraft game is copyright © Mojang AB.

This book is not authorized or sponsored by Microsoft Corp., Mojang AB, Notch Development AB or Scholastic Inc., or any other person or entity owning or controlling rights in the Minecraft name, trademark, or copyrights.

All rights reserved. No part of this book may be reproduced in any manner without the express written consent of the publisher, except in the case of brief excerpts in critical reviews or articles. All inquiries should be addressed to Sky Pony Press, 307 West 36th Street, 11th Floor, New York, NY 10018.

Sky Pony Press books may be purchased in bulk at special discounts for sales promotion, corporate gifts, fund-raising, or educational purposes. Special editions can also be created to specifications. For details, contact the Special Sales Department, Sky Pony Press, 307 West 36th Street, 11th Floor, New York, NY 10018 or info@skyhorsepublishing.com.

Sky Pony® is a registered trademark of Skyhorse Publishing, Inc.®, a Delaware corporation.

Minecraft® is a registered trademark of Notch Development AB. The Minecraft game is copyright © Mojang AB.

Visit our website at www.skyponypress.com.

10 9 8 7 6 5 4 3 2 1

Library of Congress Cataloging-in-Publication Data is available on file.

Cover design by Brian Peterson
Cover photo by Megan Miller

Print ISBN: 978-1-51073-190-5
Ebook ISBN: 978-1-51073-196-7

Printed in Canada

TABLE OF CONTENTS

THE CASE OF THE CREEPERS

THE GREAT TREASURE HUNT

Edison carefully placed a ghast tear into the awkward potion and began brewing a potion of Regeneration when Billy rushed into his bungalow.

"You won't believe it!" Billy exclaimed.

"I won't believe what?" Edison asked. Without looking up, he finished brewing and then said, "By the way, I'm done with my final batch of potion. Would you mind helping me at the stand? I have to be there soon."

"Yes," Billy replied, "but don't you want to hear my news?"

"I'm sorry, I do. What is it?"

Billy's voice was energetic, and he grinned as he spoke. "The Big Treasure Hunt is happening! I can't believe it! It's really happening!"

Billy and a few others had an idea. They wanted to

start a big treasure hunt that would take place all across the Overworld, in all other biomes. They'd invite an array of treasure hunters who would participate in a weeklong treasure hunt. When the week was over, they would all meet in Verdant Valley. There they would tally up their treasures and present the best treasure hunters with awards.

Following the event, they'd set up an area where everyone could trade, since there would be abundant treasure. Although there was a lot of support from the committee that was formed to help create the event, the planning had taken a long time, and Billy thought it would never work out. He was surprised when all of their hard work paid off and the treasure hunt was scheduled to happen. The idea that the treasure hunt was actually happening made Billy ecstatic.

Edison was thrilled for his friend. "This is the best news ever! When does it take place?"

"Next week. It's the only time when all of the treasure hunters were available. I have to get ready and prepare. I don't have a lot of time, and I need to have a stocked inventory to be able to gather treasure from around the Overworld. All of the participants have to travel to every biome and dimension."

"Even the End?" asked Edison while placing the bottle of potion into his case.

"Yes, even the End," Billy confirmed.

"Wow, I hear that's a tough dimension," said Edison.

"I've heard that too," Billy replied as he picked up

one of Edison's cases and helped him set up his potion stand in the center of Farmer's Bay. There was a small line of customers who were anxious to get their potions.

The first customer addressed Billy before he asked Edison for potions of night vision and swiftness. "Congratulations, Billy. I hear there is going to be a great treasure hunt. I am so glad you will be representing Farmer's Bay. You are an excellent treasure hunter."

"Thank you." Billy's cheeks turned red.

The next customer also congratulated Billy. He was so flustered by all of the attention that he nearly spilled a potion on his khaki shorts.

"Are you okay?" asked Edison.

"Yes," Billy said. "I guess I'm just distracted by all of the attention."

Edison said, "This is your day, Billy. You made this happen. You should be proud of yourself."

"I am, but I'm also slightly nervous," he confessed. "There are biomes and dimensions I've never been to."

"Really? I thought you'd been everywhere." Edison was surprised.

"Yes," Billy's voice shook when he said, "the End."

"I've never been there either. I do want to see End City. I hear it's incredible."

"Incredibly dangerous," said Billy.

"True, but I bet you'll get lots of good treasure there."

Billy paused and then asked Edison, "The competition allows you to bring one person as an assistant. Would you like to come with me?"

Edison knew how much this meant to Billy. He also knew that he should help Billy because Billy was such a good friend. Edison remembered when Billy was his assistant in the Alchemist Olympics and spent weeks in Edison's bungalow timing Edison as he brewed potions. Edison knew he wouldn't have won a medal if it weren't for his friend. However, he didn't want to travel around the Overworld, especially not to the End. He wanted to work at his potion stand in the center of Farmer's Bay during the day and brew potions in the evening. He was conflicted.

Billy sensed Edison's apprehension and said, "I know it's a lot to ask, but it's only a week, and think of all of the ingredients for potions you would get when we travel around the various biomes."

Edison was embarrassed that he had even paused. "Of course. I am honored you want me to be your assistant. I will make sure we have every potion we need in order to destroy any hostile mobs we encounter on the trip."

"Thank you." Billy smiled.

As Edison traded his potions for emeralds, Billy kept tabs on how many bottles were left. His blond hair fell in his face as he looked down at the bottles, calculating the remaining inventory.

"You don't have any more potions of Invisibility." Billy looked through the bottles.

"Thanks," said Edison. "We should start closing up the stand soon. It's almost dusk."

On the walk home, Billy rattled off a list of items

they needed for the trip. "We have to make sure we have armor."

"I have armor. Just give me a list of what we'll need for the treasure hunt," said Edison.

The sun was setting, and two lanky, block-carrying Endermen walked past them. The duo tried to avoid locking eyes with the creatures, but Billy must have accidently stared at one of the dark mobs, and it unleashed a deafening, high-pitched screech as it teleported toward Billy. Luckily, they were close to the shore, and Billy and Edison sped toward the water. The Endermen met their watery demise in the ocean.

As they stepped out of the water, Edison asked, "Do we have to go under the sea?"

"Yes," Billy confirmed. "We have to go to every biome."

Even though Edison had a lot of experience battling the guardians and elder guardians, he still wasn't comfortable with undersea exploration. Every time he thought about the ocean biome, he recalled the stinging pain when the rays from an elder guardian struck him.

It was nighttime as they approached Edison's bungalow. Edison pulled a torch from his inventory and placed it outside the bungalow to ward off any hostile mobs. They entered the bungalow. Billy quickly put the case on Edison's floor and left to go home. As Edison looked through his potions, figuring out what he had to brew the next morning, he heard a bloodcurdling scream, and Billy hollered, "Help me!"

2

PREPARATIONS

Edison grabbed his armor and diamond sword and rushed into the darkness to help his friend Billy.

"Edison!" Billy called out, but his voice was weak as four vacant-eyed zombies cornered him beside a tree. They were clobbering Billy, and Edison saw his friend only had one heart left. He rushed to Billy's side, slammed his diamond sword against the zombies, and splashed potion on the beasts. With one heart left, Billy avoided being hit by the zombies as he leaped toward them with his sword.

One by one, Edison and Billy successfully defeated the foul-smelling mobs, and Edison handed his friend a bottle of potion to help him regain his strength. Billy sipped the potion and opened the door to his bungalow. When Edison saw his friend safely enter the house, he hurried back to his bungalow and crawled into bed.

Although his bed was comfortable, he couldn't sleep.

Edison's mind was racing with thoughts about the treasure hunt. His heart rate accelerated when he imagined the trip to the End. He had only see the Ender Dragon once, and that was in the Overworld, when someone had unnaturally spawned the flying terror, but he had never seen the Ender Dragon in its native habitat. He heard stories about the fire-breathing dragon, how the beast would eat crystals that would increase its health, and how it was the hardest to battle. Once you beat the Ender Dragon you'd be rewarded with a trip to End City, where you would have the opportunity to get some of the best treasures, but you'd also have to battle shulkers. To calm himself down, Edison thought of all the ingredients he would gather when he went on the treasure hunt. He ran through a list of supplies he needed to create potions. Once he returned from the trip, he'd be able to brew some of the strongest potions in the Overworld.

His eyes finally closed, and Edison drifted to sleep dreaming of standing in front of his brewing stand and crafting a host of potions. He awoke with the sun shining through his window. The light was in his eyes, and he rubbed them. He looked down to see Puddles by his bedside looking for the morning meal. Edison pulled raw fish from his inventory and fed the ocelot. He could hear something rustling outside his window, so he pulled out his sword. He peeked out the window and saw Billy pulling apples from a tree.

Billy spotted his friend. "Hey Edison." He smiled and took a bite out of the apple. "Do you want me to pick any apples for you?"

"Okay." Edison walked outside and joined his friend.

Billy had a chest filled with apples, potatoes, and carrots. He looked at the chest as he spoke, "This is almost full. I want to start placing everything in my inventory. Let me know what you want. I need you to be prepared."

"We have a week," Edison reminded him.

"No, it's less than a week away, and there is a lot to do," Billy explained.

"Yes, sorry," Edison said. "Let me know what you want me to do."

"I will," Billy said and then added, "I can't help you with your potion stand today. I have too much to do."

Edison nodded his head and went back home. He had a lot of potions to brew before he opened the stand, and he had to get to work. Lately Billy had been helping him brew potions and also helped work at the stand, and Edison missed having his friend by his side. Although there were a lot of customers at the stand that morning, Edison felt lonely without his friend.

His neighbors Erin and Peyton were also his customers, and he spotted them in line. When they were ready to order their potions, Erin said, "We're so proud of Billy. Our town chose the best treasure hunter."

Peyton said, "I know he's going to make our town proud."

A woman with bright red hair stood behind them. She wore a black shirt and white pants. She asked them, "Do you have a friend in the great treasure hunt?"

"Yes," Erin smiled, "One of our very good friends is in it, and Edison is going to be his assistant. Why do you ask?"

"I'm also in it," the woman gloated, "and I'm going to win. Everyone knows that I'm the best treasure hunter in the Overworld."

"Everyone knows this, huh?" questioned Peyton.

"Yes," she smiled.

"What's your name?" asked Erin.

"Sally," she replied.

"Well, I've never heard of you," said Erin.

Sally sneered at that comment and said, "Well, you will when I win the treasure hunt. I'm sure I'll complete the entire hunt in less than the allotted week."

Edison didn't want to sell potions to this boastful person, but he knew that he had to serve all customers. "I know you think you're the best treasure hunter, but I just want to know what potions you want to buy. There is a long line of people, and I don't want to keep them waiting."

Sally ordered a range of potions from fire resistance to water breathing. She put all the potions in her inventory and didn't even say thank you or goodbye as she raced out of the town.

When the stand was closed for the day, Edison met up with Billy to plan the treasure hunt. "I saw the most irritating person today. Her name is Sally, and she's also in the treasure hunt. She claims she's one of the best treasure hunters in the Overworld."

"She is," said Billy. "It's going to be hard to win with Sally in the competition."

"I wonder who she will choose to be her assistant. I can't imagine anyone wanting to assist her."

Billy defended his competitor. "You'd be surprised. She's very well-known. People would love that job. She's an expert at finding a temple and never seems to need a map. She once came back from a two-day treasure hunt with ten chests overflowing with diamonds and emeralds. She is fearless. She's been to the End City multiple times, and she's always alone. I know many people who would love the opportunity to see her at work. If I wasn't asked to participate in the contest, I might have wanted to be her assistant."

"Well, I wouldn't," said Edison.

The next morning Edison was at his stand, but he was too distracted by the upcoming treasure hunt. All of his customers heard that he would be Billy's assistant, and they asked Edison all sorts of questions about the treasure hunt. With each question, Edison's heart raced.

"Are you going to mine for emeralds and diamonds or just search for treasures?" asked Mike, one of his regular customers.

Edison didn't know the answer.

Another customer gave him advice. "Are you going to the cold biome? If you have to travel to the Nether, you should go to the cold biome first so you could stock up on snowballs, because they come in very handy when you're battling hostile mobs."

Although Edison knew this, he nodded his head and thanked the customer for the tip.

The last customer of the day questioned him about the End. "Have you ever been to the End City?"

"No," Edison replied. "Have you?"

"Yes," the customer said. "When you're battling the Ender Dragon, the best strategy is to destroy the crystals. You have to stop the dragon from regaining its strength."

Edison's anxiety about taking part in the treasure hunt, even if he was just an assistant, dominated the rest of his week. Every day he'd make little mistakes at work, but by the end of the week, they were becoming quite noticeable. For instance, one day he gave one of his regular customers a potion of Invisibility when she had asked for a potion of Swiftness. She came back and complained. When she was running from a skeleton, she had sipped the potion and was shocked to find that the potion made her invisible! Edison apologized and refunded her all of her emeralds and then gave her two bottles of the potion of Swiftness. Although he had many mishaps, the upside was the week went by very quickly, and soon Edison was waking up and heading to the opening ceremonies for the great treasure hunt. He looked through his inventory for the hundredth time. Even though he knew he was prepared, he was lightheaded and his heart raced. He calmed himself down by going over the list Billy had provided him. Billy and Edison had checked the list several times and he had everything placed in his inventory, but he was still nervous and unsure he was prepared. As he said goodbye to Puddles and stepped outside his bungalow, sweat formed on his brow.

"Edison," Billy called out to his friend. Billy was already suited up in his armor, and he was smiling.

Edison was nervous, but he didn't want his friend to know. To calm down, he reminded himself that he had become a detective and did a pretty good job of solving crimes with Billy and Anna by his side. Like becoming a detective, this was also just a new adventure.

He stared at his door for one last time before they left. "Can you believe the next time I open this door, both of us would have completed the treasure hunt and battled the Ender Dragon?"

"I know. Isn't that awesome?" asked Billy.

Awesome wasn't the word Edison would have used. He might have chosen *terrifying*, but he looked at his friend and forced himself to smile and say, "Yeah, awesome."

3
GOODBYES

The crowd cheered as the host called all of the treasure hunters and their assistants to the stage. Edison looked out at the crowd and couldn't believe how many people were there to see them off. He saw Erin and Peyton smiling in the crowd, and he could also spot his good friends Anna and Omar.

The announcer introduced himself as William and addressed the crowd, "These are the best treasure hunters in the Overworld." The applause was deafening, but William the announcer continued, "However, they still have to follow the rules. The first rule is this: If you are destroyed, you are out of the competition. This also applies to the assistants."

Edison didn't know about this rule, and it made him very anxious.

"The second rule: You can't steal or attack any treasure hunters. If you see that someone has unearthed a treasure before you, you must search for another treasure. There are no battles in this competition."

Edison looked at Sally, and she smiled back at him.

William the announcer handed each participant a map and told them to meet back on the stage in one week. Edison could hear Sally say underneath her breath, "I don't need a week."

Edison looked for Sally's assistant, but he didn't see anyone. He looked over at Billy, "I thought everyone had to have an assistant. Where's Sally's?"

Billy pointed to a small man dressed in armor. His black hair stuck out underneath the diamond helmet. "That's him. His name is Herman. He's also a treasure hunter, but he wasn't asked to be in the competition, so Sally invited him to work with her. I guess she thinks she has a real advantage now."

Billy's voice was louder than he realized, and Sally turned around and said, "I've always had an advantage. They should just give me the award now."

"Wow, you're really confident," remarked Edison.

"Yes." She smiled. "And it's deserved."

"She's right," Herman said, and Edison was surprised that his voice was high-pitched and rather squeaky.

Edison looked at Billy. "Can you believe how confident they are?"

"Don't let them distract you," Billy warned Edison. "There are always people who think they're the best, but I believe that if you're truly good at something, you don't have to brag."

Billy studied the map. "It seems as if we have to follow their itinerary. I assume they don't want us competing for the same treasure at each location. This treasure hunt isn't about stealing from other players, but it displays how well you can unearth treasure. I'm glad they are using the same ideas and philosophies we discussed when we organized the hunt."

"Where do we go first?" asked Edison. His heart raced. He feared they'd have to start at The End. He knew that was unlikely, but you never knew what they had planned for the participants in this competition. Edison knew they wanted everyone to be challenged.

Billy pointed to the first place they had to search for treasure. "We have to go to the forest."

Edison was glad it was a rather easy biome. He was familiar with the forest and felt he could help Billy navigate. As they said their goodbyes to their friends and took their first steps on the treasure hunt, they heard someone say, "Good luck," and laugh.

"Sally." Billy was annoyed. "We have the same chance of winning as you do."

"I don't think so," said Sally, and she splashed a potion of Invisibility on her body and Herman, and they faded away.

The sun was shining, and sweat formed on Edison's brow. He was relieved once they reached the forest because the leaves shaded the sun, and the temperature was much cooler.

"What treasure are we supposed to find here?" asked Edison.

"We have to find the roofed forest biome." Billy looked at the map. "It has to be close by."

Edison recalled his last trip to a woodland mansion and the pain from fighting the illusioner. He was beginning to realize that maybe this trip to the forest wasn't going to be as easy as he thought.

Just then a wolf raced toward them, ready to attack. Edison grabbed his sword but was shocked when Billy took a bone and tamed the wolf.

"Now we have to care for this pet while we go on the treasure hunt," Edison remarked.

"It will come in handy." Billy petted the tame wolf and spoke to the animal. "I'm going to name you Lucky. You're going to bring me great luck on this treasure hunt."

Edison looked at the wolf. The path in front of them was dense with leaves, and he knew this was just the beginning. They had a long road before they found all of the treasure they needed to complete the contest.

"Is there any sign of the roofed forest biome on the map?" asked Edison.

"No," Billy said. "We have to find it ourselves. It's a part of the challenge."

Edison and Lucky followed Billy, and as he cleared a path so they could travel deeper into the woods he called out, "I found it!"

In front of them was the lush roofed forest biome. It stood out amongst the birch trees that were so tall they seemed to kiss the sky. Billy raced toward the roofed forest biome covered in dark oak trees. Edison followed closely behind and took a sip of potion to increase his health and energy before they entered this gorgeous but challenging biome. He knew that the leafy biome was dark and an easy place for hostile mobs to spawn. One of his customers once told him a story about finding a woodland mansion, but getting destroyed by two sly creepers before they could make it to the front door. Edison thought he heard leaves rustling and someone walking behind them, but he turned around and there was nobody there.

As they rushed to the biome, Edison tripped. He looked around and didn't see a branch and wasn't sure what made him fall.

"Are you okay?" asked Billy as he helped his friend up.

"Yes, I don't know why I fell," he remarked. As he spoke he could hear the faint sound of laughter.

Billy also heard the cackle and said, "I don't think you tripped. I think you were pushed."

"It looks like we have some competition," said Edison.

"I'm ready for it." Billy smiled, and the duo raced toward the roofed biome.

4

SOME CALL IT LUCK

Edison entered the biome and looked up at the roof of leaves. Large oak trees shaded their path.

"We have to find a woodland mansion." Billy paused and looked at the map.

"Isn't that really hard? You've only been to one, right?"

Billy nodded. "Yeah, remember when I got the map for the woodland mansion? That was awesome. But we have to find one now because of the treasure hunt. If we don't, we can't win."

Edison recalled the multiple mobs that dwelled in the woodland mansion. He knew Billy had to find one, but he secretly hoped they wouldn't.

Billy called out, "I found one!"

There was no mistaking the grand woodland mansion peeking out through the leafy path. Billy leaped up the stairs and opened the door. As he walked through the grand entranceway, Edison sipped a potion of Strength to help him beat the vindicator and the other mobs that lived in the woodland mansion. The minute he entered the mansion and looked down at the red carpet, he remembered the impressive foyer and the room filled with flowerpots sprouting colorful flowers, and knew he had to be prepared for what would come next. This mansion, with its wood-paneled walls, might have been luxurious, but it was teeming with terrible mobs like the vindicator, which could spawn with an enchanted iron axe, or the evoker with its fangs and vexes.

Edison took his time and inspected each corner of the mansion, searching for any one of the multiple mobs that might attack them in the dimly lit hallway. Billy did the opposite. He raced through the enormous, rare treasure–filled dwelling and searched for every diamond he could find without caring about hostile mobs.

"I found treasure!" Billy exclaimed. "Come here!"

"Where are you?" asked Edison.

"In the room that has the chest above the door. I'm on a ladder, so be careful when you enter."

Edison stood by the entrance of the room with the checkerboard floor. The walls were covered in oak fences, and Edison wondered why Billy constructed a ladder. Couldn't he have simply climbed up the fence? But then he remembered you couldn't climb fences.

Billy held onto the ladder as he opened the chest with one hand. "Can you help me?" asked Billy as he handed Edison some diamonds. "The assistant is supposed to carry all of the treasures."

"I didn't know that." Edison placed the diamonds in his inventory. "Wow, looks like you found some great treasures here."

When Billy climbed down from the ladder, they explored the rest of the mansion. Billy bolted into a room filled with construction. "We have to be careful," Billy warned. "The vindicator always spawns here, but I know there is fantastic treasure behind the construction."

Edison stared at the gray banner in the room as he followed Billy past the construction and to the treasure. He looked for the vindicator, but the hostile mob hadn't spawned.

"Got it!" Billy exclaimed. "This treasure chest is filled with emeralds and enchanted books. This is great. We are looting this mansion in record time!"

Edison raced toward Billy, quickly placing all of the treasures in his inventory. He was grateful the vindicator hadn't spawned, but he knew it was just a matter of time before they were in the middle of a battle with that enchanted axe-carrying mob.

"Okay, we're done," Billy said, and he raced out of the room and down the carpeted hallway.

"Didn't you say the vindicator spawns in that room?" asked Edison.

Billy looked at the wolf that was wagging its tail. "I told you Lucky was going to be our lucky charm."

Edison wanted to believe the dog was bringing them luck, but he knew this was slightly implausible. How could this tamed wolf stop a bunch of mobs from spawning? The idea seemed laughable. However,

Edison decided not to question Billy. He didn't want to get into any debate while they were in the woodland mansion. Edison wanted to loot the mansion and get out.

"Look—mushrooms," Billy said, entering a room with mushrooms sprouting from the ground. "It looks like a mushroom farm room." He walked toward a chest, but he sighed when he opened it. "It's empty."

Edison could hear voices as they passed a room with a large cat statue. "Do you hear that?" There was a high-pitched voice talking in the next room.

Billy said, "It sounds like Herman."

"We can't let them see us. They might try and steal our treasure," said Edison.

"That's against the rules," said Billy.

"Do you think Sally is really following the rules?" asked Edison.

"I would hope so," Billy walked into the cat-themed room, but there was no treasure. "Anyway, I think this room is usually empty. We have to find another room."

The last place they searched for treasure was in a secret room with cobblestone walls. Billy swiftly extracted the treasure. While Edison placed the blue diamonds, golden apples, enchanted books, emeralds, and other treasures in the inventory and sprinted out the door of mansion, he remarked, "You have to agree it's odd that not one hostile mob spawned in that mansion."

"No," said Billy. "I call it luck."

5

HAVE YOU SEEN A CREEPER?

"Where do we go next?" asked Edison as they exited the lush roofed forest biome.

"It says we have to go mining. There's a mine right outside of the forest, in a mountainous biome." He showed Edison the map. "I know how to get there."

The duo left the lush biome and walked uphill into the mountainous biome, where Billy pointed out the cave where they had to mine.

Edison pulled out torches for the both of them and grabbed a pickaxe. "I'm ready to mine. What do we have to find?"

Before Billy could respond, they heard unfamiliar voices in the cave. A woman with a thick French accent questioned, "Isn't it odd that we haven't seen one cave spider?"

"I know," a deep voice with a French accent replied.

"I've been mining for years, and I always find spiders in caves."

"And I haven't see a creeper in days," the woman remarked.

"Me neither," said her friend.

Edison and Billy listened. Edison said, "I told you something was off."

Billy looked at Lucky. "I'm sorry Lucky. I don't think you're the reason for the absence of hostile mobs. I think someone must be stopping the mobs from spawning so they can get treasure easily."

"But who?" asked Edison as he paced. He was getting into detective mode. He started to make a list of potential suspects, but he had only two people on the list. "I wonder if Sally and Herman have done something with the mobs."

"We can't immediately jump to conclusions. It could be anybody who is a part of the treasure hunt."

"I think I have to solve this and find out who is behind the mob disappearance," said Edison.

"But you have to help me with the treasure hunt. You're my assistant." Billy was annoyed.

"We can't let someone destroy this treasure hunt. You worked too hard to let someone cheat."

Billy agreed. The competition had been tampered with, and he had to find out who was behind it. "Yes, we can't judge a contest where someone has obviously stopped the hostile mobs from spawning."

"Is someone there?" The woman with the French accent called out.

"Yes." Edison placed the torch beside his face. "My name is Edison, and I'm here with my friend Billy."

"Billy," the woman with the French accent said, "are you a treasure hunter? I've heard of you."

The woman walked toward them; her assistant followed behind. "I'm Marie, and this is my assistant and good friend Pierre."

"We couldn't help hearing you talk about not seeing any hostile mobs. We were just in the woodland mansion and didn't see a mob there. Somebody might have stopped the mobs from spawning. When was the last time you saw a mob?" asked Billy.

Marie and Pierre both replied, "Before the competition."

Edison thought about the last time he saw a hostile mob. "I think I haven't seen one since we battled the zombies a week before the competition."

Marie said, "I saw one the day before the competition. When we were traveling here, we built a house in the swamp, and we were attacked by a witch and some slimes."

"Have you encountered any other treasure hunters?" asked Edison.

Marie said, "No, we have been on our own since the start of the treasure hunt."

They heard more voices in the distance. As they stood in the cave, another treasure hunter and his assistant walked toward them, and the two were surprised to find four people standing by the large crater on the cave's ground.

"Hi, I'm Spencer, and I'm a part of this treasure hunt." He wore diamond armor and glasses. "Is there something wrong? Aren't we supposed to be searching for treasure? I see a large crater behind you, and I want to start mining."

Marie asked the treasure hunter, "Have you seen a mob since you've been on the treasure hunt?"

"No," Spencer replied, "but we started our hunt on Mushroom Island and you don't usually find hostile mobs there."

"Well," said Billy, "we haven't seen one, and we're wondering if someone is tampering with the treasure hunt. I might speak with the committee and have them suspend the treasure hunt for an investigation."

"Suspend the treasure hunt?" Spencer was angry. "I just found so much great loot on Mushroom Island. We're not about to let someone stop this competition, right, Aaron?" The treasure hunter looked over at his assistant. The assistant nodded as he traded in his pickaxe for a diamond sword and pointed the weapon at Billy.

Billy stepped back and put his arms up in the air. "I don't want to fight. I just want this to be a fair competition."

"We do too, and we don't want some stranger telling us that they are going to cancel this competition." Spencer also took out a diamond sword and waved it toward Billy.

Marie said, "We also haven't see a mob. Look around this cave. Do you see any spiders?"

Spencer looked at the ground and walked deeper into the cave, but he didn't see any red eyes. "You're right. I usually see a cave spider."

Aaron pointed to the blue that glistened from the crater. "Look at all of those diamonds. You'd better not stop us from gathering them. You know we have only a week to gather treasure, and it's almost nightfall."

"Night won't matter on this treasure hunt because there won't be any hostile mobs. The person who stopped the mobs from spawning wants to search for treasure all the time without getting attacked," said Edison.

"Can you please stop talking about this and let us mine?" asked Spencer.

"Yeah," said Aaron. "Just move out of the way and let us mine. If you want to drop out of the competition, that's up to you, but you don't have to ruin it for everybody."

Edison and Billy watched as Spencer and Aaron mined for treasure. Marie and Pierre also started to dig deep into the crater and extract diamonds and emeralds.

"We're going to lose if we don't join them," said Edison.

"It doesn't matter," said Billy. "This treasure isn't going to count. I'm going to meet with the committee and put a stop to this competition."

Spencer crawled out of the crater and swung his diamond sword at Billy, "You aren't talking to anyone."

"You can't tell me what to do," screamed Billy. "What you're doing is against the rules."

"Nobody gets anywhere by following the rules. Listen to your friend. Mine with us and get some treasure. Stop trying to do the right thing all the time," said Spencer.

"I worked hard on this treasure hunt, and I just want it to be fair," declared Billy. "This means a lot to me. Also, I don't like to get treasure I didn't earn. It's not about simply winning to me: it's about skill."

Spencer didn't want to hear Billy lecture him on what was right or wrong. Spencer was done talking, and he leaped at Billy.

"Look!" Aaron yelled before Spencer reached Billy.

"What?" Spencer asked.

"The wolf!" Aaron said. "It's gone. I watched it disappear."

Billy looked down, but Aaron was right. Lucky was gone. "Now do you believe me?"

6

RAIN

Lucky began to bark.

"The wolf just came back. What type of game are you playing?" Spencer asked Edison and Billy, and then he looked at Aaron and said in a loud voice, "I don't trust these two. I think they're trying to trick us."

"We're not," pleaded Edison. "There is somebody who is probably using command blocks to stop hostile mobs from spawning. There must have been a glitch, and they accidently removed all of the mobs."

Marie reminded them, "We have only a week to complete the treasure hunt. I want to get my treasures, and I'd like to stop talking about people trying to destroy the treasure hunt. Honestly, it's a waste of time."

"I agree." Spencer climbed back into the crater and dug for treasure.

Edison was shocked when he saw Billy climb into

the crater and mine for diamonds and emeralds. "Billy, aren't you going to help solve this case?"

Billy hit his pickaxe against the blocky ground. "Maybe it was all a glitch. Or maybe this was a part of the contest. I have no idea, but Marie is right. We have only one week to complete the contest. If someone did use command blocks to stop hostile mobs, then we all benefited."

"Benefited?" Edison questioned.

"Okay, maybe that was the wrong word, but what I meant was that we all had an easier time getting the treasures, so the contest is fair," Billy explained as he picked up a diamond from the bottom of the crater and handed it to Edison.

Edison tried to comprehend Billy's change of heart and his logic as he climbed into the crater and joined his friend.

"We've found a great mine. There are so many diamonds here," exclaimed Marie.

"I know." Spencer handed Aaron another diamond.

Edison worried that they weren't getting enough diamonds, and he hoped Billy wasn't upset because they were sidetracked for a portion of the contest. Edison was mining the crater, extracting diamonds and emeralds, when he saw Marie and Spencer leave the mine.

"We have more than enough diamonds. We have to find our next treasure," Marie told Pierre.

"Great." Pierre asked, "Where are we off to next?"

Marie replied in a whisper, and Edison couldn't make out her destination. As the other two teams exited the cave, a thunderous boom shook the ground, and they could hear the rain pounding down outside the cave.

"Help!" Marie screamed.

Edison rushed outside, but Billy stayed behind. Edison called out to his friend, "Aren't you going to help?" But there was no reply.

When Edison reached the exit, he saw five skeletons surrounding Marie and Pierre as they tried to defeat the bony beasts with their diamond swords. Edison put his pickaxe away, took out his diamond sword, and joined Marie and Pierre in battle.

As they leaped at the skeletons, Edison could feel an arrow pierce his unarmored arm, and he cried out in pain as he lost a heart. Edison knew this meant there were more skeletons behind them. He called out to Billy, but his friend didn't appear.

Marie destroyed two skeletons and Pierre obliterated the remaining three as Edison raced toward the new crop of skeletons that attacked them.

"How many are there? I can't even count," said Pierre.

"At least twenty," Marie said. "I don't know what we're going to do."

Edison reached into his inventory and pulled out a bottle of potion and splashed it on the skeletons, but it only weakened them and didn't destroy them.

He called out, "Billy! Come here!"

Billy finally raced toward his friend. "And we thought there weren't any hostile mobs?"

"I know," said Edison. "This is awful."

Billy blurted out a plan. "You splash the potion, and I'll strike them with my sword."

With Marie and Pierre by their side, they were able to annihilate some of the skeletons, but every time they destroyed a skeleton, a new batch would walk toward them. The terrain was flooded, and Edison's feet were sinking into the soggy ground. He shivered as he splashed potions on the skeletons. Although he felt invigorated as he watched the skeletons grow weak after being doused with his strong potions, he also knew that he had a limited amount of potions and didn't want to use them all up on this one battle. When he splashed the skeletons with the remaining bottle of potion, the sun came out, and the skeletons disappeared.

"Well," Marie said, "now we know there are hostile mobs."

Billy asked, "What happened to Spencer and Aaron? Did the skeletons destroy them?"

"I don't know," said Marie. "When I came out, they were already gone."

"I wonder where they went," said Edison.

"I did see purple mist," remarked Pierre. "Perhaps they went to the Nether."

"We don't have time to worry about Spencer and his assistant," Marie remarked. "We have to go." To avoid letting Edison and Billy know where she was traveling to next, she quickly splashed a potion of Invisibility on Pierre and then on her body, and they were gone.

"I think it's strange that Spencer disappeared and suddenly we were attacked by skeletons," said Edison.

"Edison"—Billy didn't look up from his map as he spoke—"I don't want to play detective during the treasure hunt. I've been waiting for this hunt for such a long time, and I don't want anything to ruin it."

"Okay," Edison said. "I will try to stop playing the role of detective and will focus on being your assistant. I know how much this means to you."

Billy pointed at the map. "The next place we have to go is the Nether. Did you pack obsidian?"

"Of course." Edison pulled the obsidian out from his inventory and began to craft a portal. He wanted to prove to Billy that he could be a good assistant.

When the portal was finished, they stood together on the small platform. The duo was covered in purple mist as they emerged in the hot and harsh Nether.

Before they had a chance to adjust to this hostile dimension, Billy screamed, "Watch out, you're about to fall into lava."

Edison looked behind him. There was a large lava river, and he was just one step from falling back into it. As he sprinted from the lava lake, a cluster of ghasts flew above them. Edison was about to deflect a fireball when an arrow struck his shoulder. He slammed his fist against the fireball and then turned back to see who had shot the arrow, but nobody was there.

7

NOT IN THE NETHER

"**O**uch!" Billy said as slammed his fist against a fireball.

"Was it hot? Did you get burned?" asked Edison.

"No." Billy tried to look back, but he couldn't. He was too busy battling the ghasts that flew overhead. "I am being struck by arrows."

"Me too," said Edison. "But I have no idea where they're coming from."

The duo used their fists to destroy the ghasts with their own fireballs, and once the final ghast was annihilated and the sky was clear of hostile mobs, they sprinted deep in the Nether in search of the person who was attacking them with arrows. They traveled along the lava lake and up a bridge, and although they had a great view from the bridge's platform, they didn't see anybody.

"Even if they used a potion of Invisibility, we'd be

able to see their bow," Billy remarked as they stood on the bridge.

"I see a Nether fortress." Edison pointed to a small structure behind an obsidian pillar.

"Let's go." Billy climbed down the bridge, and they raced toward the Nether fortress.

As they made their way toward the fortress, two zombie pigmen walked by them. They were able to avoid eye contact and didn't provoke the pigmen, but something caught the pigmen's eyes, and they became hostile. Edison and Billy watched as the pigmen lunged at something they couldn't see and grew more and more frustrated.

"We're not alone," said Billy.

The zombie pigmen focused on Billy and Edison and raced toward them with their swords. Edison struck one of the pigmen with his diamond sword, but the mob was stronger than he imagined. No matter how many times he sliced into the pink-and-green speck-led belly of the foul-smelling undead pig, he couldn't destroy it.

Billy slayed his pigmen with two strikes from his sword, and this impressed Edison since he was slowly losing his battle with the sole pigman. "Help!" he shouted to Billy.

Billy ripped into the pigman, destroying the beast with a few hits from his diamond sword, and the pig-man dropped a gold ingot on the ground. "Wow," Billy said as he picked up the gold ingot and the gold nugget his zombie pigman had dropped. "They drop very valuable treasures. Put these in your inventory. We can show them to the committee and will see if they can count toward the treasure we are gathering for the contest."

As Edison placed the treasure in his inventory, he felt another arrow pierce his arm, and he screamed out in pain. "What is going on? Who is shooting arrows at us?"

Billy replied, "I don't know, but I'm sure we'll find out when we try to get the treasure from the Nether fortress."

Edison pulled a bottle of potion from his inventory and took a sip. Then he handed it to Billy. "Take this. We need all the strength we can get before we enter that fortress. I think we're going to be battling a lot more than blazes and magma cubes."

With a full health bar, the duo used their renewed energy to sprint toward the fortress. Approaching the grand fortress, they were stopped when a group of blazes flew above the entranceway, carefully keeping watch by the fortress.

"You have snowballs, right?" asked Billy.

"A bunch," confirmed Edison.

The blazes shot a slew of fiery balls toward them as they pulled out their snowballs and simultaneously leaped from the explosive ammunition. Billy threw a snowball at a yellow blaze. The ball landed on one of the blaze's many limbs but didn't destroy the tricky beast. Edison also threw a snowball at the blaze, striking the blaze's face.

Edison loved the feeling of a cold snowball. The heat from the Nether was weakening him, and it was refreshing to have an ice-cold snowball in the palm of his hand. He didn't want to let go of the snowball, but he had to aim it at the blaze that flew in front of the fortress entrance.

Pow! The blaze was destroyed, and Edison was confident he could destroy the other blazes. He slammed another ball into a blaze's warm yellow body, obliterating the mob.

"We only have one left," said Billy. His voice was upbeat, and he was hopeful this battle with the blazes would be over soon.

Edison pulled a snowball from his inventory and threw the ball at the blaze, destroying the final beast. They picked up the blaze rods that dropped to the ground.

"We did it," Billy said as he hurried through the entrance of the Nether fortress. But as he entered, Billy could hear a familiar noise. Something was bouncing around, and it sounded like magma cubes.

"We'll never get to the treasure if we have to battle these magma cubes," Billy said as he pulled out his diamond sword and followed the sounds from the cubes.

Edison spotted the red-, orange-, and yellow-eyed cubes in the center of the Nether fortress and used his enchanted diamond sword to slice into the flesh of the large, slimy, dark cube, which then broke into smaller cubes. Billy fought the smaller cubes while Edison broke another larger cube into pieces. Edison picked up the magma cream when all of the magma cubes were destroyed.

"Let's hope this place hasn't been looted yet," Billy said as he searched for treasure.

Edison quickly gathered soul sand and Nether wart and placed it in his inventory.

"Come on, Edison." Billy was annoyed.

"You promised that I could gather ingredients for potions, and you know I never get to travel to the Nether," explained Edison.

"Well, make it fast. I am going to look for treasure," said Billy.

Billy dashed down a corridor, and as he turned, he spotted a chest. "I think I found treasure!"

Edison rushed to his friend and watched as he opened the chest, which was filled with iron horse armor. He placed the goods in his inventory. "I'm so glad we were the first ones to get the treasure from this fortress. Now that battle with the blazes and the magma cubes seems worth it."

"True," Billy said as he raced through the fortress in search of more chests. He hoped he'd find diamond horse armor next. He searched in each room until he found a chest. "I found another one."

He opened the chest and pulled out obsidian. Edison placed the precious block in his inventory. He felt another arrow pierce the side of his arm, but this time when he looked back, he saw a familiar face standing behind him.

8

SUSPECTS

"This is my treasure. Hand it over," the squeaky, high-pitched voice called out.

"No way," said Billy as he closed the chest and pulled out his diamond sword. "We got this treasure first, Herman."

"I was here before you," declared Herman.

"Where's Sally?" asked Edison.

"She dropped out of the competition," he explained. "I'm taking her place. I am going to win without an assistant."

Edison thought it was very strange that Sally dropped out of the competition when she was so confident that she'd win. However, he didn't have time to come up with any theories about Sally's whereabouts because within seconds, Herman had darted toward him and torn into every unarmored limb, weakening

Edison. Billy handed Edison some milk and then struck Herman with his diamond sword.

After finishing the milk, Edison pulled a potion of Harming from his inventory and splashed it on Herman, leaving him with only one heart. Billy pointed out Herman's weakened state. "You only have one heart left. We can destroy you, which will instantly eliminate you from the contest."

Edison said, "He's already eliminated. He broke rule number two."

"What was rule number two?" asked Herman.

"No cheating or battling other players," said Edison as he held his sword against Herman's small body.

"Tell us where Sally is," demanded Billy.

"I'm right here." Sally giggled as she spoke.

"I'm going to report you two," said Billy.

"It's your word against mine. Who says they're going to believe you?" Sally laughed as she aimed her bow and arrow and struck Billy's arm.

Billy wanted to strike Herman, but he didn't want to destroy him. He knew that could get them all kicked out of the competition. He said, "I just want to continue with the competition. I don't want either of us to get kicked out. Can you guys just leave us alone so we can spend the rest of the week treasure hunting?"

Sally paused. "So you're going to let us get away with this? I mean, we did attack you."

Billy knew this wasn't wise, but he was having such a good time searching for treasure, and the competition had barely begun. He said, "This is a warning. If I catch you trying to attack anyone else, I will report you to the committee."

Edison didn't wait for a reply. He grabbed Billy, and they sprinted from the fortress and crafted a portal back to the Overworld. As they emerged in the center of the cold biome, they saw Lucky racing toward them with his tail wagging. Billy leaned down to pet the wolf.

"Do you think we made the right decision?" asked Edison.

"I don't know, but I didn't want Sally ruining the entire competition," said Billy.

"I know, but she is probably going to attack another player. We have to report her," said Edison.

"Why do we always have to be the people who make sure everyone is doing the right thing? Why is this always our responsibility? Why can't we just think about ourselves? We want to be a part of this competition. Why do we have to care about anyone else?"

Edison understood what Billy was saying, but he knew that it was also important to look out for others. "I know we've played detective before and solved many cases in the Overworld, and I understand that it's a lot of work, but we can't just let bad people get away. If we do, we are just as guilty as they are."

Billy didn't want to debate, especially when he knew what Edison was saying was correct. He looked up at the sky. "It looks like it's almost dusk. I think we should build an igloo."

"I will help you build the igloo, but you have to promise me that if we encounter any other players who are breaking the rules of this competition that you will make sure you TP to the committee and report them," said Edison.

Billy reluctantly agreed as he put down the base for the igloo. "Okay, I will report them. I hope this was the only incident because I really want to complete the treasure hunt and travel to End City. I can just imagine all of the treasure we will find there."

With all that had been going on during the competition, Edison had forgotten about the trip to the End, and as he helped construct the igloo, his mind raced with thoughts of the Ender Dragon. He tried to recall the tips he had received from one of his customers. He remembered to attack the crystals because that would stop the dragon from replenishing its energy.

As they placed the door and window on the igloo, the sun began to set. Edison looked out the window of the igloo onto the dark and icy landscape and said, "I don't see any hostile mobs on the horizon."

"Do you think someone has done something to the hostile mobs again?" asked Billy.

"I don't know." He looked over at Lucky and said, "Maybe it's just luck."

As he said those words, the wolf disappeared.

"What just happened?" asked Billy, "Where's Lucky?"

"I don't know," said Edison. "He just disappeared."

Billy got up out of his bed and looked out the window. "There aren't any hostile mobs. I don't even see a Polar Bear."

"I think someone is tampering with the contest," said Edison.

"And you want us to report it." Billy searched the small igloo for Lucky, but he couldn't find the tamed wolf.

"Yes," said Edison. "We can TP to the committee and let them know what happened in the Nether and also that your wolf vanished in front of our eyes."

"But I just want to finish the week. We'll find Lucky when the contest is over," said Billy.

"I don't think we can wait that long." Edison was annoyed at his friend. "You promised me that if anything else happened you'd report it."

"But—" Billy was about to plead his case, but he was interrupted when Anna spawned in the center of the cozy igloo.

"Anna," Billy asked, "what are you doing here?"

"The Overworld is in a state of chaos, and we need your help," she told her friends.

9
FACTS OR RUMORS

"Anna, what's going on?" asked Edison.

"There are no mobs in the Overworld," Anna explained, "and it's causing a horrible effect on the universe."

"We think someone is tampering with the hostile mobs in order to win the treasure hunt," said Billy. "We were going to report them, but I wanted to go on with the hunt. I feel bad that I didn't report them, but I was having so much fun being a part of the competition."

Anna said, "But the competition is so small in comparison to what is happening across the Overworld. There are no mobs, which means there is no meat, and people have been stealing from farms in the middle of the night when nobody can see them. This lack of mobs has created a famine across the Overworld. The food shortage is intense, and people are starving. Do you have any food in your inventory?"

Edison looked through his inventory and found some chicken. "I have a piece of chicken."

"You'd give me a piece of chicken? That is so rare. You can trade chicken for almost anything. I can't take anything that valuable from you," said Anna.

"I want to give it to you. You're a good friend." Edison handed her a piece of chicken, but she refused to take it.

"I will take anything else, but I won't take a piece of chicken. Do you have a piece of bread or a cookie?"

Billy pulled a piece of bread from his inventory. "Is this good?"

Anna ate the bread in one bite. "Thank you. I was starving. This happened so quickly, nobody had time to prepare."

"Now we have to find the person or people responsible for this, because we can't let them destroy the Overworld," said Billy.

"Do you really think it's all happening because of the competition? Or is this something bigger? Is someone trying to ruin the Overworld?" asked Anna.

"It seems like too much of a coincidence," said Billy. "There have been a few treasure hunters that haven't followed the rules of the competition, and I think they could be behind this attack."

"Are you talking about Sally and Herman?" asked Edison.

"I also wonder about Spencer and Aaron. I find it odd that they disappeared before the rainstorm," said Billy.

"Yes, the rainstorm was the brief period when mobs returned, but nobody could hunt because there was a skeleton attack," said Anna.

"We had to battle skeletons too," remarked Edison. "This can't go on. We have to put an end to this. We can't let the people of the Overworld starve."

Billy didn't want to express his disappointment for the competition coming to an end when the Overworld was in such an awful state, but he had to admit that he was very sad to leave the treasure hunt. "We will find the people behind this. Anna, are you going to help us?"

"Of course. We always work together." She smiled. "And now I can think because I have eaten. You have no idea how awful it is to have nothing to eat. I couldn't think about anything else but getting some food into my stomach. My health and food bars were empty."

Edison and Billy looked through their inventories and began to rattle off the food. "I have lots of meat, fruit, and bread," said Billy. Edison had a fully stocked inventory, which included milk and potions to help them regain their strength.

"We should be fine for a while, but we should definitely conserve what we have and eat wisely," said Edison.

Anna suggested, "Maybe we should go back to Verdant Valley and meet with the committee. If this does have something to do with the treasure hunt, they should know. If they cancel the hunt, the person behind this might let mobs spawn again."

"That sounds like a good idea. Now that there aren't any hostile mobs, we can head there now since we won't get attacked by the mobs that spawn in the night," said Edison.

"They have to be a part of the competition. If they weren't, they'd see what they were doing to the Overworld," said Billy.

"Maybe they want to destroy the Overworld. Maybe this is the biggest criminal we've ever had to find," suggested Anna.

"I hope not." Edison's voice was shaky.

"We have to TP there now and talk to the committee," said Billy. "I know William, who was the announcer at the competition, is in charge of everything now that the hunt has begun. I'm sure he'll want this information."

"He's staying in the castle, right?" asked Anna.

"Yes," Billy replied. "Let's TP back to the castle."

The trio TPed back to the center of Verdant Valley and emerged in front of the castle, but walking inside and searching for William wasn't as easy as they imagined.

"Oh no!" Billy cried as he watched a gang of zombies rip the door from the castle. Everywhere they looked, there were hostile mobs. The streets were flooded with skeletons, zombies, and even spider jockeys.

They each pulled out an enchanted diamond sword from their inventory, but they didn't know where to begin the battle.

10

MISSING

The people of Verdant Valley were too weak to battle, and Edison watched as the townspeople were instantly destroyed by a single skeleton's arrow or by a zombie lunging at them.

Billy spotted his friend Omar in the midst of a battle with three skeletons. Omar leaped at the skeletons with his diamond sword.

"Omar," Billy called out to his friend as he raced toward him. "It's Billy."

"Help!" Omar's voice was faint. "These mobs just spawned. I've never seen anything like it, and I only have one heart left."

Billy rushed to his friend's side and struck the skeletons until they were annihilated. He picked up the dropped bones and handed Omar a potion for healing.

Omar drank the potion in one gulp and said, "It

looks like every mob in the Overworld has spawned in the last two minutes."

Billy scanned the battleground. Every mob in the Overworld was battling the townspeople except one. Where were the creepers? Two block-carrying Endermen walked through grassy Verdant Valley while a sea of skeleton's arrows flew past them. Billy tried to avoid locking eyes with the lanky mob, but Omar accidently did. One of the Endermen unleashed a high-pitched shriek and teleported to Omar.

A zombie crept up behind Billy and put an arm on his shoulder. Billy struck the zombie with his sword, slicing into the fetid flesh. The zombie was stronger than Billy expected, and it took at least four hits before the undead beast was obliterated.

"Run to the water in the moat!" Billy screamed to his friend as Omar raced from the Endermen.

Billy raced to his friend, who stood in the moat next to the bridge that led to the castle Omar had constructed.

Omar said, "We are too weak to battle these mobs." He walked out of the water once the Endermen were destroyed by the fatal liquid. "I don't think we can battle too much longer. I hope this stops soon."

"Stick with us," said Billy, "We have full inventories. We can help you battle these mobs."

"Battle these mobs? We'd need an army to defeat all of these mobs. We need more help," Omar said as he turned around and struck a zombie with his diamond sword.

The foul-smelling zombies seemed to spawn in

groups of twenty, making the fight against them incredibly challenging. The smell from the zombies was sickening, and Billy tried to annihilate as many as he could while holding his breath.

Edison and Anna raced over to help them battle, but Anna was struck by too many arrows, and she was destroyed. Edison sprinted toward Anna's home. As he opened the door, he saw his friend spawn in her bed.

"Take this." He handed Anna milk and a slice of bread. "You need your energy."

"Did you happen to notice that every mob from the Overworld is here, but there aren't any creepers?" she asked as she sat up in her bed.

A zombie ripped Anna's door from the hinges, and the duo bolted through her small living room and slammed their swords into the belly of the zombie with oozing flesh that broke into Anna's home. The zombie was destroyed, but the battle wasn't over. A spider jockey spawned in front of Anna's door and shot arrows at them. The arrows flew from the skeleton's bow as the bony beast rode atop the spider. The spider's red eyes glowed in the darkness, and Edison took a deep breath as he struck the spider with his diamond sword while trying to dodge the arrows that shot toward him. Edison slammed his sword into the spider, and the skeleton was unsteady and fell off the spider. Anna hit the skeleton's arm with her sword, weakening the beast but not destroying it. As Anna battled the skeleton on her own, Edison obliterated the spider.

Anna and Edison picked up the drops from the

spider and the skeleton, but when they looked up, they found themselves surrounded by twelve zombies.

"This is impossible," Edison said, as he pulled out the last bottle of potion he had in his inventory. He splashed the zombies, but there were too many, and the potion was useless. He tried to fight back, but the horrid-smelling zombies clobbered Edison. He awoke in his bed. His heart raced. He had been destroyed. Did this mean they lost the competition? He felt awful. He had let his best friend down. He had to meet with the committee and explain that this was a special circumstance, and they should be allowed to continue with the treasure hunt.

The sun shone through his window. Puddles meowed, and he handed the ocelot the last of his raw fish. When Edison fed Puddles, he realized passive mobs had returned. He rushed to the window. Farmer's Bay was incredibly peaceful.

He pulled an apple from his inventory and ate because he needed to restore his energy for his trip to Verdant Valley to meet with the committee. He had to explain why Billy should be allowed to stay in the treasure hunt. Edison thought about what he'd say when he approached the committee. He'd list all of the cases they solved together and how Anna, a fellow detective, reached out asking for help. As he stared out the window, he imagined himself standing in front of the committee. He was confident that he could get Billy back in the hunt. From the window, he could see Peyton and Erin walking down the road. He rushed outside and called out to his friends. "Peyton! Erin!"

He met his neighbors on the path near the town farm. Edison was shocked when he saw the state of the town farm. The farm had been emptied. It was devastated. There were no more crops left, and the flourishing farm was almost gone. There weren't any new crops ready to sprout from the ground. The apple trees had not a single apple hanging from the leaves. It was just dirt.

"Can you believe what happened to the farm?" asked Peyton. "People stole all of our crops when the passive mobs vanished and the famine started."

"It's awful," said Erin. "We are going to work on rebuilding the farm today, but I hope it's not a fool's errand. I don't want to spend the day trying to seed the farm and then have people destroy it again."

"It's okay, we can rebuild now," said Edison. "Passive mobs are back. My ocelot, Puddles, is in my house."

"That's true," said Erin, "but who knows what is going to happen next? It seems like every day there is some new challenge. It's very hard to live in this type of environment."

"Yes," Peyton agreed. "I spent the last few days starving. It's been awful. I'm glad the passive mobs are back though. I was able to get some chicken this morning. I really missed eating meat."

"I know, everything that happened was awful," said Edison. "I promise I'm going to find out who is behind all of this and stop these attacks."

Like many of the other promises he made in the past, Edison hoped this was a promise he could keep.

11

BACK ON THE HUNT

Billy, Anna, and Omar were talking to William when Edison entered the castle. Edison could hear Billy say, "It looks like everything is back to normal. I think I should return to the treasure hunt."

William nodded. "Yes, but please come back to Verdant Valley if something happens again. We have to get to the bottom of this, but like you suggested, we will have you investigate when the competition is over."

Billy was thrilled to get back to the treasure hunt. He saw Edison. "Did you hear the good news? We can go back to the treasure hunt."

Edison wanted to ask Billy if he mentioned that things weren't totally back to normal, that nobody had seen a creeper in a while. However, he knew how much this competition meant to Billy, and he was glad that everything seemed to be back to normal in the

Overworld, with the exception of the disappearance of the creepers.

Anna and Omar wished Billy and Edison good luck. The duo left to get back to the hunt. Edison asked, "Where do we go now?"

"The jungle. We have to get treasure from a jungle temple, but it's not close by. We have to travel to get there." Billy showed Edison the map.

The trip to the jungle temple led them into the swamp. Edison wasn't a fan of the swamp. He realized he'd used all of the potions in his inventory and asked if he could stop back at his house to get more.

William overheard Billy and Edison and remarked, "No, you can't refill your inventory. You can only use what you packed before you left for the hunt."

"But I used up my potions battling these mobs," explained Edison.

"Everyone on this hunt had to battle hostile mobs, and they aren't able to replenish their inventory. The reason the committee is letting the competition continue is only because everyone had the same challenges," said William.

Edison understood what William was saying, but he didn't necessarily think it was correct. He was certain there was somebody on the treasure hunt who was using command blocks to tamper with the competition, and he bet they didn't have an emptied inventory. Edison knew continuing with the competition without any potions would leave him exposed and incredibly vulnerable. Before he had a chance to state his reasoning for why he should be allowed to replenish his supply, William said, "You're lucky I am letting you guys stay in the competition. You were destroyed, Edison, and that meant that both of you were immediately eliminated from the treasure hunt. But I made a special allowance because I know both you and Billy were instrumental in trying to help stop the madness that is taking place in the Overworld."

Edison knew it was pointless to continue asking William for anything else, and he followed Billy and Lucky on the path toward the swamp and tried not to think about the fact that he didn't have any potions.

"Maybe I can brew something," Edison suggested as they reached the swampy biome.

"Do you have a brewing station?" asked Billy.

"No," Edison replied, "but what else can we do? I'm really worried that we're going to be destroyed. I'm an alchemist. I rely on potions for everything, and you know that I'm not the strongest fighter. I don't want to ruin this treasure hunt for you."

"You aren't going to ruin it for me. We will just have to rely on other skills to get us through this hunt," said Billy.

The sky was growing dark, and Billy suggested they build a house in the swamp. As they placed the foundation for the makeshift house, they could hear *bounce, bounce, bounce.*

"Slimes," Edison said as he put a wooden plank atop another to create the wall of the home.

"Well, this will be our first battle without potions.

Luckily, it's an easy mob," Billy pulled out his diamond sword as he raced toward the sound of the slimes. He found them on the edge of the swampy lake. He tried not to fall in as he sliced into the boxy slimes with his diamond sword.

Edison rushed over to help his friend, but he was nervous as he watched the sunset and the full moon loom above them in the dark sky. A bat flew close to his helmet, and he ran as fast as he could until he reached Billy.

"I'm almost done battling the slimes," Billy said as he plunged his sword deep into the slime and it broke into smaller slimes. Edison annihilated the smaller slimes with a few whacks from his sword.

"We have to finish the house before more hostile mobs spawn," said Billy.

As they raced back to finish the home, they could hear a creepy laugh in the distance.

"A witch!" said Billy.

The purple-robed witch lunged toward them. She clutched a potion in her hand, and the duo raced away from her. They didn't want an ounce of the potion touching their skin. Billy hid behind a tree and traded in his sword for a bow and arrow and aimed at the witch. The arrow seemed to take forever before it landed in the witch's stomach. This attack infuriated her, and she picked up speed as she raced in their direction with her potion in hand.

Edison aimed his bow and arrow at the witch, but the arrow just hit her hat and didn't affect her health. As the witch approached them, they sprinted further away, shooting as many arrows as they could. Using trees and the darkness to hide from the witch, they were barely able to weaken the creepy creature.

Bounce, bounce, bounce. The sound of slimes was heard behind them. With the witch in front of them and a crop of slimes moving closer, they were cornered.

"If only I had potions," said Edison.

"You can't think about that now." Billy was upset. They had to focus on survival and not dwell on their weaknesses.

As they shot arrows at the witch, they listened to the sounds of the bouncing and knew the slimes were inches away. Edison shot an arrow that pierced the witch's chest, and she was destroyed.

With renewed energy from their victory, they turned and sliced into the slimes, ripping the bouncy beasts into pieces and carefully destroying all of the smaller slimes that bounced on the ground.

"We have to finish this house. The mobs have seemed to return to normal. It was much easier when they didn't exist," said Billy.

"Maybe it was easier to get treasure, but look what it did to the Overworld—people were starving," said Edison as he quickly placed a window and a door on the house they swiftly constructed on the shore of the swampy lake. They used the light from the full moon and a couple of torches to see in the dark night.

"I know what it did to the Overworld, but it really made treasure hunting fun," said Billy as he walked into the house and crafted two beds.

Edison climbed into his bed and pulled the covers over himself. He wished Billy a good night, and closed his eyes. He wished that when he opened them, the Overworld would continue to be back to normal. As he drifted off to bed, he dreamed about a creeper. He hoped he wouldn't see them only in dreams and he'd finally be able to see one in the Overworld. Once he spotted a creeper, he would know everything was okay.

12

IN THE JUNGLE TEMPLE

The sun shone through the small window and woke Edison and Billy. Billy fed Lucky. Edison looked out the window and said, "It looks like everything is still okay. Lucky is here, so we have passive mobs, and the swamp looks like the swamp."

"That's good," said Billy. "We're not far from the jungle temple. After we get the treasure from the jungle temple"—he paused as he studied the map—"it looks like we go to the desert, the ocean biome, and then to End City."

"Already? We're almost at End City? I thought that would be the last place we go." Edison wasn't looking forward to a visit to the End.

"The treasure hunt is almost over," Billy reminded him. "It's only a week long."

The duo set out with Lucky, and after passing through a meadow, they were in the middle of the jungle. The biome was thick with leaves, and Edison stopped to pick a melon growing. He bit into the watery melon. "Have a melon, they're amazing."

Billy picked one and ate it. His mouth was full when he spoke. "I don't want to waste any time. I want to find the treasure."

Edison pulled a few more melons from the ground. "We should take these in case something happens again. We should have extra food on hand. I know you want to rush to the treasure, but we have to make sure we're prepared."

"True," Billy said and filled his inventory with melons. "But we really have to get going now."

They looked up at the light sky as they made their way through the dense landscape. Billy pointed to a jungle temple behind some leaves.

"Great," Edison exclaimed, but he stopped when he heard voices. "Do you hear that?"

Billy listened. The duo could hear a high-pitched, squeaky voice. Billy said, "It sounds like Herman," and then added, "Listen, Edison, I don't want to battle them. I just want to get the treasure."

"Billy, I'm not sure we are going to be able to get the treasure that easily," said Edison.

As they darted into the jungle temple, they saw Sally standing by the entranceway with a red parrot perched on her shoulder.

"Where do you think you're going?" asked Sally.

"This is the next stop on our map," said Billy.

"You can't attack us again. If you do, I promise I

will TP to Verdant Valley and tell William that you are causing problems on the treasure hunt," said Edison.

"Am I attacking you?" asked Sally.

"You guys have to calm down," said Herman.

Billy walked toward the door of the jungle temple, but Sally blocked it. Billy exclaimed, "What are you doing? I want to enter the temple."

"Why? I already looted it," said Sally softly as she looked at the bird.

"You can't stop me from looking in the temple," said Billy.

"Why should you waste your time? Go to the next location listed on the map. You lost this temple," she told him.

"I'm going to report you for stopping us from entering the temple," declared Edison.

"Tattletale," Sally said, and she moved out of the way. Billy and Edison entered the jungle temple and raced to the bottom floor.

"The trapdoor is still closed. She wasn't telling the truth," said Billy.

"That isn't too surprising, but I don't understand why she let us in here. Or why she didn't loot the treasure. She is just standing out front with a tame parrot. That doesn't sound like the Sally that I've seen," said Edison.

Billy didn't want to talk about Sally. He was carefully solving the puzzle and unearthing the treasure without unleashing the arrows that were often launched when he removed the treasure from a jungle temple. "I did it!" Billy exclaimed when he finally got the treasure.

He opened the first chest. "Saddles," Billy called out as Edison put them in his inventory. The second chest had diamonds, and the final chest had bones.

When all of the treasure was placed in Edison's inventory, Billy said, "We have to get out here, I don't trust Sally."

They zipped toward the exit. As they took their first steps outside the door, they heard a familiar voice with a heavy French accent demanding, "Give me all of your treasure."

Billy pulled out his sword and waved it at Marie. "No way!"

Edison followed Billy and grabbed his sword and leaped at Pierre.

"You better give us what you just took from the jungle temple," Marie rubbed her sword against Edison's unarmored arm, scratching him.

"I am going to report you," declared Edison.

"Why are you doing this? The hunt is almost over. Why are you ruining it for all of us?" Billy asked them.

They were all stunned when Sally emerged from a leafy path with the red parrot still perched on her shoulder. "Marie, leave them alone. And let the best player win."

13

DESERT DISCOVERIES

"**W**hy did Sally defend us?" asked Edison as they reached the desert.

"I don't know. I can't figure it out. There is definitely something going on, but we'll solve all of this when the contest is over." Billy wanted to get to the desert and the ocean biome, then head to the End, which would complete his weeklong journey.

Edison hoped they'd be able to finish the treasure hunt without any more incidents that had the potential to destroy the Overworld. He was still upset that he hadn't seen a creeper in days. He believed that once he saw a creeper, he'd know everything was okay.

"Okay, I hope we get to finish the hunt," said Edison.

"Stop saying things like that." Billy was annoyed. "We have to remain positive."

The sandy desert was in sight, and Billy picked up his pace, tearing through the arid biome with Lucky tailing him. A calm lake ran through the hot biome, and Edison felt his body temperature rise. His face was drenched with sweat, and he asked his friend to slow down. "It's too hot to run," he pleaded.

"We have to run. I think I see a desert temple." He pointed to a sandstone structure beyond a cluster of sugar cane growing by the water.

Edison saw the palatial desert temple. The massive temple looked like a pyramid, and the orange pattern engraved on the side of the temple's towers awed him. The impressive structure, located on the sand, seemed even larger in the barren landscape. Billy was far ahead of him, and Edison tried to catch his breath as he loped behind Billy and Lucky. Billy raced into the temple in search of treasure. He was deep within the temple when Edison walked through the door.

"Billy," he called out, but there was no response. Edison searched for the dog, but as he searched through each room, the temple was empty. His voice was louder. "Billy!"

"Who are you looking for?" someone asked him.

Edison turned and saw Spencer and Aaron. They were smiling. "The treasure hunt is over," Spencer announced.

"Where is Billy?" Edison demanded.

"You'll be with him soon enough," Aaron said.

"This is against the rules. You can't attack another player," said Edison.

"Rules." Spencer laughed. "Nobody ever wins by playing by the rules."

"That's not true," said Edison. He swung his diamond sword at Spencer.

"See?" Spencer smirked as he spoke. "Even you're breaking the rules. You're attacking me when I don't even have my sword out. I can report you."

"You have taken my friend. This is self-defense," explained Edison, and he pointed his diamond sword at Spencer.

"Help!" Billy called out. His voice was faint, but Edison recognized it.

"Tell me what you've done to Billy," Edison screamed.

"We'll take you to him," Spencer said as he walked down a hall in the airy desert temple and into the main room. The blue wool block in the center of the room was broken, and Edison knew that meant the treasure had been found. Spencer led Edison through the block and into the treasure room. The chests were emptied, but there was a pressure plate that had yet to be activated. If the plate was broken, TNT would explode, and they would be destroyed.

Marie and Pierre were holding their swords against Billy and threatening to activate the TNT.

"You're all working together?" asked Edison.

"Maybe," Marie replied, "We've already claimed this treasure, and we want you to leave the desert. Of course, not having treasure from the desert means that you'll probably lose the competition, but that's your problem."

Billy didn't want to get caught in a battle with these

players, and he told Edison that they should follow their directions and leave.

Edison wanted to report these corrupt players, but he wasn't going to announce his plans. He agreed to leave the biome with Billy, and they made their way out of the desert temple.

As they walked toward the shore, where they would ingest a potion of Water Breathing and search for treasure in an ocean monument, Billy said, "There is too much corruption in this treasure hunt. I knew the hunt wasn't going to be easy, but I didn't think the players would gang up on us. I feel like everyone is working together and we are the odd men out."

"We wouldn't want to be a part of their team. They're cheaters," said Edison.

Billy knew Edison was correct, but he also felt excluded from the treasure hunt. It seemed like everyone had a plan that he didn't know about. Everybody except Sally. He wasn't sure where Sally fit in to all of this, but he was going to figure it out.

As they stood on the shores of the ocean and took out their bottles of potion, before they swallowed their first gulp, they heard someone call out, "Stop!"

14

THE CASE OF THE CREEPERS

"Sally," said Billy.

"And Herman," added Edison.

"We have to tell you something." Sally raced toward them.

Both Billy and Edison were suspicious of their motives. Billy demanded, "Tell us now. We don't have time to mess around."

"We just passed a cave that was carved into the side of a mountain that isn't far from here. In the cave, we saw a room filled with command blocks. We waited to see if the person who was using them would show up, but they didn't," she confessed.

"Show us where it is," said Billy. As these words fell from his lips, he wanted to suck them back in, but he couldn't. He realized this might be a trap, and he had fallen for it.

"I'm so glad you want to see it. I'm going to tell

74 *The Case of the Creepers*

William about it," said Sally. "I've been watching Marie and Spencer and their assistants, but I haven't traced either of them back to the command blocks. I am at a loss."

"Why are you asking us for help?" Edison questioned. He was suspicious of Sally and took out his diamond sword.

"You're not going to hit me with the sword?" asked Sally.

"Yes," Herman added in his squeaky high-pitched voice. "Sally is innocent."

Edison wasn't going to bring up Sally's behavior earlier in the competition when she tried to attack them. He just said, "It's getting dark, and I am worried that hostile mobs will spawn. It's always good to be prepared."

When they reached the cave, Lucky vanished. Billy called out for his dog, but it was gone. "I bet someone is using the command blocks now."

As they entered the cave, the group was flooded with arrows. They couldn't see who shot them, but the only thing Edison remembered from the attack was the pain, and then he woke up in his bed.

He awoke, but Puddles wasn't by his bedside. He could hear somebody at his door.

"Edison?" Billy called out. "Are you there?"

"Yes." Edison got up from bed, but he was still groggy. He picked a slice of bread from his inventory and chewed. It still hurt to chew. Billy walked into the bedroom and Edison said, "I'm sorry, I guess we lost."

"Guess so," Billy said. "I thought it was a trick, but I just wanted to believe Sally, and I wanted to see who was using the command blocks."

"Let's talk to William and tell him what happened," said Edison.

"Did you see who attacked us?" asked Billy.

"No," Edison replied. "The instant I walked into the cave, I was hit with arrows, and I couldn't see anything."

"But I'm sure Sally was behind this. She was trapping us so she could have somebody attack us," said Billy.

"We aren't certain of that," Edison reminded him. "We can't get her in trouble. She might have been trying to help the treasure hunt."

"I am sure she's the one who is destroying the treasure hunt, and I am going to tell William." Billy was infuriated that they were even discussing this. They should have been meeting with William to have Sally removed from the competition. He wanted them to have her deactivate her command blocks and be punished.

"We can't place blame on her. We have no proof," explained Edison.

Billy was about to speak when Sally and Herman rushed through the door. Sally announced, "We have to meet with William."

"Sally, what are you doing here?" asked Billy.

"Herman and I were destroyed by the people behind the command blocks, and since I have a history of causing trouble, I wanted you guys to come with me when I meet with William."

Herman said, "Sally is innocent."

"I never said she wasn't," said Edison. "We will go with you."

As they left Edison's bungalow and were about to head to Verdant Valley, they stopped when they saw that the path in Farmer's Bay was cluttered with creepers. The green explosive mob marched through the streets. Billy and Edison called to their friend Peyton, but it was too late. A group of creepers ignited themselves, and Peyton was destroyed.

Billy looked at Edison. "You said the world would be okay if we just saw a creeper. What do you think now?"

Edison's mouth was agape as creepers crammed into each other as they went down the path beside the Farmer's Bay farm. "If they all explode at once, can they destroy a house?" asked Edison.

"I don't know," Sally replied.

"And I don't want to find out," added Herman.

The green creepers silently traveled down the path, and the gang was afraid to use their diamond swords for fear that they would set off an enormous explosion.

"I've never seen that many creepers," said Edison. "I wish Puddles was here, because creepers are afraid of ocelots."

"Passive mobs must still be gone," said Billy, "but I don't think Puddles would be strong enough to scare off all of the creepers."

"We have to go back to the mountain and see who is manipulating these command blocks," said Sally.

"How are we going to get there?" asked Billy. "How can we get past the creepers?"

Sally looked out at the green monsters that were creeping toward them. "I think we should TP to William in Verdant Valley."

Edison thought this was a great idea. He also wanted to find his friend Anna because she was always helpful when solving a case, and they needed to figure out who was behind this creeper attack.

"Okay," said Billy. "Let's TP."

As they collectively TPed to Verdant Valley, they spawned in the center of the castle, but it was empty.

"William," Sally called out.

"The castle seems empty." Billy darted throughout the castle searching through all of the rooms. "The committee isn't here."

"Why aren't there any people here?" asked Herman.

"The Overworld is in a worse state than we thought," said Sally.

"We should go find Anna," suggested Edison. "She might know what happened."

As they raced out the door of the castle, a loud explosion shook the castle floor. From the windows, they could see smoke fill the streets of Verdant Valley, and they looked out to see every inch of Verdant Valley covered in creepers.

"Creepers are everywhere," said Billy.

"We have to find Anna," Edison repeated.

"How?" asked Sally.

"We can't leave her in this creeper-invaded world," said Edison.

"We have to protect ourselves," said Herman.

"We have to pull the bridge up so they can't travel over the moat," suggested Billy.

The gang raced toward the bridge, but the creepers had already reached the foot of the bridge, and by the time they were able to lift the moat, it was too late. They didn't have enough time. Creepers filled the bridge and were entering the castle.

"Oh no," said Herman as they stood by the bridge. "We're trapped. They're already in the castle."

"They could blow it up." Billy's voice cracked.

"Do you think they could really do that?" questioned Edison as he looked down at his diamond sword. He used to think the diamond sword was the most powerful weapon, but now it felt useless. There was no way he could destroy all of these creepers with one diamond sword. He wished he had potions in his inventory, but it was bare.

"I have a plan," said Sally confidently.

Edison hoped it was a good one.

15

PLAYER VS. PLAYER

"Let's make a portal to the End," she said. "It's the only way out of here."

"What? That's crazy. We can't travel to The End now. We have to help the Overworld," said Edison.

"What else can we do?" demanded Sally. "We can't leave the castle. In a few seconds, this room will be filled with creepers, and we'll all be destroyed, only to respawn and get destroyed all over again. At least if we go to the End, we might find some treasures."

"How is that going to help anyone?" asked Billy. "Of course I want to travel to the End and go to End City, but now isn't the time. We have to stay here and fight."

There wasn't any time left to debate. The creepers entered the room, and Billy dashed toward them with his diamond sword, but they exploded. Billy was caught in the middle of two exploding creepers, and he lost the last of his hearts.

"Billy!" Edison called out, but his friend was gone.

Edison slammed his sword into two creepers before he was also caught in an explosion, but he was overwhelmed by the creepers and lost the battle. He respawned in his bed and was surprised to see Puddles beside him. Edison got up and was walking to the window when he heard Billy crashing through his door.

"The creepers are gone," exclaimed Billy.

"And passive mobs are here." He pointed at Puddles, who meowed.

"We have to TP back to Verdant Valley to find out what happened to the others," said Edison.

The duo TPed into the castle, but the castle was empty. They called out for William, but he didn't respond.

"We should leave," suggested Billy as he clutched his diamond sword. He wanted to be prepared. He never knew who would appear outside in Verdant Valley.

Edison followed his friend over the bridge that was once filled with creepers and stared at the sky. "It's almost night. We have to find them quickly."

The streets of Verdant Valley were empty. "Where is everybody?" Billy was worried.

"I don't know, but we should go to Anna's house. We have to find her." Edison hurried in the direction of Anna's home.

When they reached her door, Sally called out to them. "Guys, I have some crazy news."

"What?" asked Billy.

Sally said, "William is behind all of these attacks."

"Really?" questioned Edison.

"She's right," Herman confirmed. "We have reason to believe he is the one who is using the command blocks."

"But why?" asked Billy. "He was the one who we chose to head up the competition. Why would he want to ruin it?"

As they spoke to Sally and Herman, Anna opened her door. "Billy! Edison! I'm so glad you guys are okay."

"For now," said Edison.

Billy and Edison walked inside the house, but they stopped when they saw William standing in Anna's living room.

"What is going on?" questioned Edison.

William paced around the small living room. "Someone is trying to destroy the competition, and everyone thinks it's me, but I'm not the one responsible for all of this."

"Why do people think it's you?" asked Billy.

Sally and Herman shot through the door of Anna's home. Sally announced, "It's William. We found you. Now confess. Tell us why you're destroying the competition."

Edison and Billy waited to hear his response, but William stood in silence. Billy demanded, "Answer us. Tell us why people think you're guilty. We chose you for this job because we thought you'd be the fairest person to run and judge this competition. Why would people believe that you're behind its destruction?"

William still stood frozen in silence.

Kaboom! A loud explosion shook Anna's home, and the gang raced to the window to see what had exploded.

"The creepers are back," Anna cried. Verdant Valley's streets were jam packed with creepers, and every inch was covered in green.

"This is even worse than before!" said Sally.

Edison and Billy looked back at William. They wanted to tell him to stop this madness, but when they looked for him in Anna's home, they couldn't find him.

"Where did he go?" questioned Billy.

"I don't know," said Anna as she ran through the small home. A thunderous boom sounded in the distance.

Sally cried out, "It's a lightning storm! The creepers are charged!"

"We have to find William!" screamed Billy. "We have to stop this!"

Herman's high-pitched, squeaky voice was hardly audible amongst the backdrop of creeper explosions. "I think I know where we can find him."

16

THE SHOW MUST GO ON

"Where?" asked Edison as creepers detonated outside and smoke filled the living room.

"We have to go to the cave," said Herman.

"But how are we going to get there?" asked Edison.

Sally confessed, "I know what to do. You have to TP to Spencer."

"What?" asked Billy.

"He's in the cave," explained Sally. "Come with me."

The group TPed into the cave and emerged into the center of a battle.

"Stop the command blocks!" William hollered as he struck Spencer with his diamond sword.

Aaron stood guard by the command blocks, as Spencer and William dueled. William saw the gang and called out weakly, "Help me!"

Billy swung his diamond sword at Aaron. "I'm in charge now."

Aaron splashed a potion of Harming on Billy, weakening him. Edison lunged at Aaron, slicing into his arm as he splashed more potion on Billy. A drop of potion landed on Edison's arm, and he was weakened. Anna rushed into the battle and struck Aaron with her sword, leaving him with one heart.

"Shut the command blocks down," screamed Anna, "and do it now."

Creepers silently crept into the cave.

"Where's the creeper spawner?" demanded William. "You have to shut it off."

Sally said, "I know where it is." She bolted outside, and Herman followed her.

With only one heart left, Aaron was vulnerable. He stood by the command blocks, pleading, "Stop, I will destroy them."

"We'll help you." Billy banged his sword against the command blocks.

The creepers still flooded the cave, and William and Spencer were surrounded by the green mobs. While Billy and Edison slammed their swords, breaking the command blocks, they could hear an explosion. They turned around to see William and Spencer caught in the blast as they destroyed the final command block.

Despite the absence of command blocks, the creepers were still entering the cave, and Billy, Edison, and Anna battled the green horde that invaded the dimly lit cave. A pair of red eyes stared at them from the corner of the cave, and Anna leaped toward the spider, whacking it with her diamond sword. "I never enjoyed

destroying a spider as much as I just did," she remarked
as she sprinted toward the creepers, ready to destroy the
last of this intense hostile invasion.

Edison noticed the creepers weren't entering the
cave, and there was a smaller group of creepers clus-
tered by the entrance. "Sally must have deactivated the
spawner."

Two creepers crept up beside Spencer and destroyed
him with an explosion. Edison annihilated one of the
final creepers that lurked in the cave as he said, "Both
suspects got away. What are we going to do?"

Sally entered the cave. "I have shut down the
spawner," she announced.

"And we destroyed the command blocks," Billy
said as he annihilated the final creeper.

"Now we have to go find Spencer and Aaron," said
Edison.

Before they could come up with a strategy to find
the suspects, William raced into the cave.

Sally leaped at William with her diamond sword.
"You are a criminal."

"I'm not," said William. "I can explain."

"I saw you with Spencer and Aaron. You were
standing here by the command blocks." Sally inched
closer to William.

Anna called out in William's defense, "Don't
threaten him. Let William explain. He's innocent."

"Really? Then why did I see him with them?"
demanded Sally.

"I was trying to stop them. I found out about the

command blocks from Marie and Pierre. They TPed to the castle and informed me that they found the command blocks."

Edison couldn't believe Marie and Pierre would be the ones to report the command blocks. "Marie and Pierre tried to rob us. Why would they report someone who was doing something wrong?"

William didn't have to answer that question. Spencer entered the castle with Aaron trailing behind him. Spencer said, "They were trying to win the competition, but they knew I had all of the power. They wanted to bring me down."

"Power?" questioned Edison. "Trying to ruin the Overworld isn't power. It's pathetic."

"Yes," added Billy. "Power is trying to win the competition on your own, through skill, not by cheating."

Sally said, "I agree. When the contest first started, I wanted to win so badly, I resorted to desperate measures, but then I realized I should see if I could win honestly."

"How nice," Spencer said. "But in the end everyone lost."

William remarked, "I am glad you confessed, Spencer. You and Aaron are not only out of the competition, but you will be held responsible for the destruction that occurred in the Overworld."

Anna told them, "You caused a famine. It was horrific."

Spencer and Aaron didn't apologize. Instead Spencer asked, "What about Marie and Pierre? Are they in trouble too? They stole from players."

"Yes," William replied. "They will also be punished and asked to leave the contest."

"The contest is still happening?" asked Billy.

"I will let you and Sally compete for the title on a trip to End City. Whoever extracts the most treasure there will be declared the winner."

Billy suggested, "I think I should go as a team with Sally, Herman, and Edison. Do you want to do that Sally?"

"You want to treasure hunt with me?" Sally was stunned.

"Yes, I think we're both good treasure hunters, and if we stick together, we'd find more treasure than if we go at it alone," he said.

"That's true," said Sally, "but this is a competition. Don't you want to see who is the best treasure hunter in the Overworld?"

"I did. In fact, I was one of the founders of this treasure hunt, but when I saw how it made people act, I wasn't very happy with the hunt. I think the best way to end this competition is to finish it together," explained Billy.

Sally smiled as she pulled out an Eye of Ender, and with a big grin she said, "Let's travel to the End."

17
WE'RE ALL IN THIS TOGETHER

Edison's heart raced as he entered this new dimension. Standing on a pillar in the dark, he waited for the famed Ender Dragon to appear. He was armed with a bow and arrow and a sword. However, his most important assets were the three people beside him. It was nice to know that he wouldn't have to battle this hostile, fire-breathing dragon that resided in the End on his own.

Roar! The dragon breathed fire at them as the gray-winged beast flew toward their legs, and Billy struck the beast with his diamond sword. The dragon's wing hit Billy, diminishing his hearts. Edison shielded himself behind a pillar, recalling what his customer had told him, and aimed his bow and arrow at the crystals. With a careful shot, he destroyed the crystals.

The dragon charged toward them, shooting an Ender charge at the group. Herman was unable to escape the hit from the Ender charge, and a purple cloud surrounded him as he slowly felt the effects from the potent charge. The charge's mist contained a harmful and possibly lethal aroma that diminished hearts. Herman was left with only one heart, and Sally tried to hand Herman a potion to regain his strength while she dodged another Ender charge.

Billy slammed his sword into the belly of the dragon as it flew past them, but he was barely weakening the beast. Edison watched as the dragon flew in the direction of the crystals, and he tried to destroy the crystals before the dragon had time to eat from them. He shot the arrow and cheered when he watched the arrow break the crystals.

Herman sipped the potion and then pulled his bow and arrow from his inventory and shot arrows at the dragon. The barrage of arrows that flew from Herman's bow impacted the powerful dragon, and the beast was weak. When Edison destroyed the final crystals, he was confident they would annihilate this challenging mob boss. Billy and Sally ripped into the dragon's flesh, destroying the dragon.

"It's time to go to End City!" Sally exclaimed.

"I've never been there before," said Billy.

"We haven't either," said Herman.

"I hope we find it," added Edison. He didn't want to admit that he had his fill of excitement and would rather head back without visiting End City. He was simply happy that they had destroyed the Ender Dragon.

"Look!" Sally pointed to a large castle in the

distance. She marveled. "It's right there." Sally charged toward the dark purplish city.

Edison was the slowest of the group, and he was the last to enter the city. Billy and Sally were already inside a building made of purpur blocks. He could hear Billy call out, "Treasure!"

Edison could barely see in this city, with End rods lighting this grim landscape, he found himself squinting, but it didn't help him see. He clutched a torch as he walked through the creepy castle. He kept a close eye out for Endermen and any other mob that might lurk around the dimly lit structure.

As Edison entered the room filled with treasure, he felt something hit his unarmored arm. Within seconds he was floating in the air. He had no idea what was happening to him, and he called out, "Help!"

"What's the matter?" asked Sally as she raced out of the room. When she realized Edison had been attacked by a shulker, she called out, "Billy! Herman! Edison has been injured, and we will be too if we don't get out of here."

It took a while for Edison's feet to reach the ground, and he was still a bit wobbly as he walked out of the castle. When he reached the door, he was struck by another shulker and was suspended in air.

"Help!" he cried again.

"Oh no!" Billy rushed to his friend's side as the effect from the shulker wore off.

"We have to watch out for those shulkers," said Edison. "They hide in purpur blocks, so they are almost impossible to find."

Sally exclaimed, "An End ship!"

Edison was in awe of the massive purple ship docked at the end of a pier with a dragon head on the bow.

Sally took out an Ender pearl. "This is how we get onboard." She looked at her friends. "Are you ready, guys?"

They nodded, and Sally threw the Ender pearl. Once onboard, Edison stared at the brewing stand. He wanted to create potions, but he knew he was there for Billy. Even so, he quickly grabbed the two potions of healing on the stand. Once he placed the potions in his inventory, he felt a lot more confident. He missed having potions with him. He knew how to use them, and they were a part of how he was able to help and heal.

Edison followed the gang down the stairs and into the famed treasure room. When he reached the room, all three of his friends were floating in midair. The second he put his foot down on the obsidian ground, he was also struck by a shulker and began to levitate above the treasure room. He took a sip of the potion and then passed the bottle along to his friends, and they all landed on the obsidian ground. Herman was the first to attack the shulker, striking the beast when it popped out of the purpur block.

Billy and Sally opened the chest and in unison called out, "Wow!"

"What's in there?" asked Edison.

"Elytra," replied Sally.

Billy added, "Now we can fly when we're back in the Overworld."

"That's such a rare find," said Herman. "This is incredible.

With the treasure hunt complete, the gang crafted a portal back home.

18

INVENTORY

The town of Verdant Valley was in a celebratory mood. There was a feast upon their return, and a large crowd greeted them.

William stood on the stage. "About a week ago I wished these people well as they went off on their treasure hunt. A lot has happened since then. When I first stood on this stage, I was sending people out to compete against each other. Now the treasure hunters have returned, and they aren't competing with each other, but they have worked together to extract some of the most valuable treasures in the Overworld."

Sally and Billy took out the treasures they found during the treasure hunt. Everyone marveled at the finds, and people cheered when they showed the audience the elytra. Sally put on the elytra and coasted above the audience. When she landed on the stage, she looked at Billy. "You're next." Billy put on the elytra and flew. As he looked down at the crowd, he realized the treasure hunt didn't turn out how he expected. He was still upset that Spencer and Aaron had caused such suffering through the competition, but he was also glad that he made new friends. He never thought he'd end the competition with Sally at his side.

William thanked everyone for attending the treasure hunt and invited the group, along with Anna, to a celebratory meal at the castle.

"What happened to Marie and Pierre?" asked Edison.

"They went back to their town. They broke the competition rules, but they weren't like Spencer and Aaron," said William.

"Sally, thank you for letting us know Spencer and Aaron were behind this," said Billy.

"You know, you'd make a good detective," added Edison.

"Maybe you'd like to join us on our next case," said Anna.

Sally smiled. "Next case? Sign me up."

Edison was glad to be home, but he wasn't ready to solve another mystery. Although he knew it was just a matter of time before he had to help the Overworld, he was going to spend this afternoon celebrating his friend Billy, one of the best treasure hunters in the Overworld.

The End

WANT MORE MINECRAFT ADVENTURES?

Read the Unofficial Overworld Adventure series!

Escape from the
Overworld
DANICA DAVIDSON

Attack on the
Overworld
DANICA DAVIDSON

The Rise of
Herobrine
DANICA DAVIDSON

Down into the
Nether
DANICA DAVIDSON

The Armies of
Herobrine
DANICA DAVIDSON

Battle with the
Wither
DANICA DAVIDSON

Available wherever books are sold!

DO YOU LIKE FICTION FOR MINECRAFTERS?

Read the
Unofficial Minecrafters Academy series!

Zombie Invasion
WINTER MORGAN

Skeleton Battle
WINTER MORGAN

Battle in the
Overworld
WINTER MORGAN

Attack on
Minecrafters
Academy
WINTER MORGAN

Hidden in the
Chest
WINTER MORGAN

Encounters in
End City
WINTER MORGAN

Available wherever books are sold!